KB147624

김연하 시선집

A Selection of Poems by Kim Yeon-ha

영겁의 강

The Eternal River

시 김연하 · 번역 우형숙

Written by Kim Yeon-ha
Translated by Woo Hyeong-sook

문학사계

발간사

　계곡마다 꽁꽁 얼었던 물이 풀리며 추위에 움츠렸던 나무들이 겨울눈을 오동통하게 살찌우고 꽃필 준비를 하며 한파를 피해 겨울잠을 자던 개구리가 깨어나 꿈틀꿈틀 나올 준비를 하는 계절입니다.

　이번 시선집 제호는 『영겁의 강』으로 정했습니다. 제가 지금까지 쓴 15권의 시집 중에서 60편을 선별하고 한글시를 영문으로 번역하여 함께 엮었습니다.

　본시는 지금까지의 인생 경험을 소재로 시 창작을 하면서 조약돌 및 구두 등 1,170편의 시를 썼습니다. 저의 시는 거창한 소재가 아니라 소박한 꿈을 실현하려는 마음으로 아름다운 강산을 바라보며 희망을 찾아 제1부 「조약돌」 제2부 「백두대간」 제3부 「먼 산」 제4부 「인생의 길목에서」순으로 편집했습니다.

　시작품 번역은 쉬운 일이 아닌데 오랜 시일 동안 성의를 다해주신 우형숙 번역가와 제 시집을 출판해 주신 문학사계 황혜정 발행인에게 감사의 말씀을 드립니다.

　끝으로 이 시집을 읽는 독자 여러분의 공감을 기대합니다.

2021년 1월 1일
고담古潭 김연하金連河

Preface

The frozen water melts in every valley. The trees, which were pinched with cold, are ready to bloom, along with weight gain by the winter snow. Frogs, which hibernated to avoid the winter cold, wake up, ready to come out of their holes.

The title for this poetry book is The Eternal River. To publish this book, I selected 60 poems from my 15 poetry books, and the poems were translated from Korean into English.

I have written 1170 poems, focusing on life experiences as material, including pebbles, shoes, etc. My poems don't have stunning material, but they have a simple dream come true, with the beautiful scenery for hope. I divided this book into the following four parts: Part 1 Pebbles, Part 2 Baekdu-daegan Mountain Range, Part 3 A Distant Mountain, Part 4 On the Corner of My Life.

Though poetry translation is not easy, Woo Hyeong-sook willingly translated my poems into English for several weeks. I'd like to commend her very highly on this. And I would like to thank Publisher Hwang Hye-jeong profusely for the publication of this poetry book.

Lastly, I truly would like my poems to evoke sympathy from readers.

January 1st, 2021
Kim Yeon-ha (pen name: Godam)

차례 Contents

제2부 · 백두대간
Part 2 · Baekdu-daegan Mountain Range

제3부 · 먼 산

Part 3 · A Distant Mountain

제4부 · 인생의 길목에서
Part 4 · On the Corner of My Life

제1부 · 조약돌
Part 1 · Pebbles

조약돌 1

얼음이 녹아 흐르는
세찬 물살에
새알처럼 다듬어지고

소용돌이 속에
만나고 부딪치며 깎이는
인연의 여울목에서

주름살 깊어갈수록
삶의 잔재미가 모여
세월 따라 둥글게 둥글게
사랑의 윤선(輪線)을 그려가네

Pebbles 1

Ice melts, and the icy water runs;
in the swift current
pebbles become round like birds' eggs.

When meeting in a whirlpool,
the pebbles bump against each other,
sharpening up their relationships.

As their wrinkles become deeper,
they tend to get more subtle pleasures.
As years go by, they mark the wheels of love
on their round surfaces.

구두

새로 구입한
구두 뒤축이 길에 쓸리고
반듯하게 닳지 않고 비스듬해져
길들이기를 해가네.

아무리 발끝을 모아 걸어도
언제 풀렸는지 모르게
밖으로 튕겨 나가
한쪽으로 비스듬한 것을…

질곡 없는 삶 어디 있으랴
살아가며 후회 많은 날들
삶의 중심이 기울어져가고
깜짝할 사이 흐르는 세월

골반이 기울면 기울수록
뼈가 사근거리다 주저앉은 듯
낡은 뒤축과 밑창이 어긋난 채
저녁노을처럼 기울어가네.

Shoes

My new shoes
have worn down at the heels.
The heels are slanted, not right up,
so I try to make the heels perfectly straight.

However hard I try to walk, focusing on my tiptoes,
I soon walk slantwise again.
With my unmindful steps
I walk, leaning on one side.

Where's the life without the ups and downs?
In our lives, there is a lot to regret.
The center of my life is getting lopsided,
and the years go by so quickly.

The more tipped my hips are,
the more painful I feel in the joints.
My shoe heels and soles wear down unevenly,
getting more tilted like the setting sun.

민들레

외로이 떠돌던
홀씨 하나
길섶에 날아들어 뿌리내렸다.

거친 발길에
짓밟히고 뭉개져도
아픔을 딛고 살아온
끈질긴 고난의 삶,

슬픔은 별이 되고
괴로운 가슴을 지우며
노란 꽃으로 피어나
여물어 가는 생명의 씨앗,

꽃등에 실려
어느 언덕 날아가도
고운 얼굴로 다시 피어나

작은 가슴 가득히
초록빛 향기 뿜어내며
온 천지에 번져 나가리.

A Dandelion

Having wandered all alone,
a dandelion spore
took root at the edge of a road.

Though it was trampled and crushed
by the footsteps of passers-by,
it got over the pain
and survived considerable hardship.

Its sorrow became a star;
easing the sufferings,
it became a yellow flower
that has the seeds of life.

It'll be carried, on a flower petal,
away to a certain hill,
but again it may bloom pretty.

From its small green chest,
its fresh scent will emanate,
spreading everywhere.

강마을

물안개 자욱한 강마을에는
복사꽃 향내음처럼
젊은 날의 추억이 살아
강으로 흘러 흘러가네.

연분홍 복사꽃잎이
초야의 꿈처럼 싱그러워지는 날
그 길을 걸어가면
아직도 못 다한 속삭임이 있다네.

햇빛을 품어 안던
꽃바람 부는 강물에
외로운 초승달 창에 들면
무수히 많은 별들이
강물에 잠기고

강물이 보이는 언덕에
연분홍 복사꽃이 반사하여
돌아서는 길목에서
발목을 애타게 잡아매네.

A Riverside Village

A riverside village, veiled in mist,
evokes memories of my youth,
just like the scent of peach blossoms;
but the memories flow into the river.

The pink petals of peach blossoms
look fresh like the dream that I had at a rural home.
When I walk along the path,
I recall the whispers that we didn't finish.

Embraced in the sunlight,
the gentle breeze blows over the river;
when a lonely moon is seen outside the window,
myriads of stars in the sky
seem to submerge into the river.

On the hill overlooking the river,
pink peach blossoms, reflected on the river,
don't allow me to leave there
when I turn around and go.

조약돌 2

오랜 세월 흙에 묻혔다가
흐르는 개울가에 잠수하며
역경의 길 걸어가네.

모나고 투박한 돌들이
여울목에서 긴 세월 뒹굴다가
깎이고 부딪히는 아픔…

우글거리는 욕망 속
마음 비워 살아가는 인생처럼
고난 뒤에 행복을 찾듯

먼 길 숨 가쁘게 달려와
뼈를 깎는 고통을 견디며
당차고 둥글게 살아가네.

Pebbles 2

Buried under the ground for a long time,
pebbles are submerged in a brook,
living their tough lives.

The stones, once too sharp and tough,
have rolled so long in a swift current,
suffering from the pain of cutting and bumping...

In a strong desire,
they seem to find happiness after adversity,
by trying to empty their minds.

They've come a long way at a fast pace,
by coping well with excruciating pain;
now they get along well with each other.

외딴집

고즈넉한 강변에
자리 잡은 아담한 집에서
살고 있는 할아버지 할머니

집을 에워싼 울타리에
복사꽃이 만발하고
둑 아래엔 모래가 반짝이네.

연어가 회귀하는 계절
건강한 어미와 아비로 성장해
돌아오는 아들딸 기다리며

하늘엔 흰 구름 떠가고
어둠을 쫓는 눈부시게 밝은 빛
마냥 행복해 하는 할머니 할아버지.

An Isolated House

In a cozy house
by the lonely riverside,
a grandfather and his wife live there.

Peach blossoms are in full bloom
over the fence around their house,
and the sand glitters under the riverbank.

When salmons return to where they were born,
the aged couple wait for their kids,
who will also become healthy fathers and mothers.

White clouds drifting across the sky,
the light so bright as to remove darkness,
the aged couple are elated at all of these.

망향가

춘풍이 수목을 빗질하고
구름 없는 밤 떠오르는 달이
나뭇가지에 노닐던 곳

밤이면 밤마다
도란도란 나누는 이야기
배꽃 하얗게 넋 놓고 웃는
모습에 취하는데

뻐꾹뻐꾹
뻐꾹새가 망향가를 부르고
술에 취하여 별을 보고
골목에 스러지며

조상 대대로
옹기종기 모여 살던 땅
유년의 뜨락 소꿉동무 어디 가고
하늘만 높푸른가?

A Nostalgic Song

A spring breeze blows, like combing trees;
the moon rises on a cloudless night,
and it plays on the branches of the trees.

Every night,
people talk with each other in whispers,
being captivated by the white smile
of pear blossoms.

Cuckoo cuckoo
a cuckoo sings a nostalgic song;
a drunken person looks at the stars,
lying down on an alley way.

For generations
people lived there together.
The sky is still high and blue,
but where are my childhood friends?

달그림자

달빛이 방문을 열면
낯익은 모습으로
저만치 걸어가는 그림자 하나

눈을 감으면
다정다감한 얼굴로
꿈처럼 다가오는 그 모습

인연 엮어놓고 떠난 뒤
밝은 달이 고갯마루에 올라
나뭇가지에 걸려있는데.

소쩍새는 밤새 울어도
새벽은 오지 않고
님 그림자만 가슴에 있네.

The Moon's Shadow

Moonlight opens the door of my room.
Then, a shadow, so familiar,
is seen to walk there.

When I close my eyes,
a friendly face still haunts me,
like I'm in a dream.

After making relations with me, my love left me.
A bright moon is between the boughs
on the peak of the mountain.

A scops-owl hoots sadly all night long,
but dawn doesn't come.
Only the shadow of my love is in my heart.

독백

앞만 보고 달려오다 뒤 돌아보니
무한경쟁의 높은 벽
태산처럼 보기만 해도 어지럽고
어깨의 짐 너무 무거웠네.

시(詩)는 나의 새로운 희망
더러 혹자는 허접하다 말하며
고루한 말이라 핀잔을 줄지 몰라도
나는 어디서나 하고 싶은 말…

무심코 떠오르는 영감은
마음속에 집을 짓고
밖으로 창을 열면
자유 천지가 한눈에 보여
표현이 되고 시가 되네.

발끝까지 저린 새빨간 그 아픔
한가지씩 하늘에 묻고
이제 남은 시간 한 걸음씩 쉬엄쉬엄
좋은 시 한 편 남기고 가려네.

Monologue

After I ran looking forwards, I look backwards now.
O I was on the way for unlimited competition.
The wall was as tall as Mt. Taesan, making me dizzy;
I lived with so much burden on my shoulders.

Writing poems is my new hope;
some people may say that writing is a trifling thing,
for they regard it as an outdated idea.
But anywhere, I want to say about my hope.

A flash of inspiration
sets up a nest in my mind;
when I open up my mind,
the liberal world enchants me,
ready to come out as a poem.

Let me bury in the sky
even the pain that made my feet get numb;
slowly moving step by step for the rest of her life,
I want to leave a good poem before I go.

어머니의 산

파란 하늘 우러르는 모성
가슴 깊이 들어와 사랑스럽게
우리를 보듬어 감싸 안는다.

칠흑의 밤에는 움츠렸다가도
새벽이면 불어오는 훈풍에
서둘러 잠에서 깨어나며

산의 등줄기를 따라
푸르른 생명의 맥이 흐르고 흘러
꿀꺽꿀꺽 젖을 빠는 하루

새벽이면 포동포동 젖살 올라
여명의 빛으로 아기처럼 뽀얗게
슬기롭고 아름답게 빛난다.

Mother's Mountain

Looking up towards the blue sky,
the maternal instinct of the mountain
enters our hearts and embraces us warmly.

On a pitch-dark night, the mountain draws back,
but around dawn, it hurries to wake up
in a warm gentle breeze.

Along the ridge of the mountain
there is fresh vitality of life;
as if suckling from it, I receive vigor today.

At dawn, the mist rises like chubby baby cheeks;
in the early morning sunlight,
it shines white and pretty like a baby.

시심詩心

시(詩)는 선(禪)의 세계로
순수한 마음속에 내재해 있는
상상의 나래를 편다.

삶의 맑은 거울인양
은은하게 채색된 수채화처럼
감동을 선사한다.

쓰라린 고통보다
더욱 심한 진통을 통해 얻은
호수처럼 맑은 마음

자연의 참모습 터득해
아름다움을 발견하는 감성이며
톡톡 튀어 오르는 생각…

A Poetic Turn of Mind

Immersing me into a world of meditation,
a poem lets me indulge in a flight of fancy
that has been deep in my mind.

A poem is like a clear mirror of a life;
it touches me quietly yet so deeply,
like a watercolor painting of a subdued color.

A poem seems to be born through birth pangs
rather than bitter anguish,
as I see it showing such a mind as clear as a lake.

A poem needs sensibility to find beauty
from a distinctive way of thinking,
by realizing the true face of nature...

꿈

누군가 가슴에 희망을 품고
한여름 달리다 흘린 땀 씻어주는
얼음처럼 시원한 바람 같이

가슴에 꿈을 담고 달리다
뒤돌아보고 다시 도약하려 하면
바위가 길을 막고 덮치려하듯

허덕이며 거친 파도를 헤쳐
마음 달래고 힘 모아 살아온 세월
어둠 속에도 열매는 익어 가리.

A Dream

Someone, with a hope, runs in midsummer,
wishing for a wind, as cold as ice,
that would wipe the sweat off his brow.

He runs with a dream in his heart.
But when he looks back and then leaps again,
a huge rock happens to be in his way, blocking him.

Going his way through rough waves,
he has steeled himself to survive a dreary life.
Even in darkness, all fruits will turn ripe.

숫돌

아버지는 목수였다.
숫돌에 물방울을 떨어뜨려
무딘 대팻날을 문지르면
제 몸 깎으며 날을 세웠다.

잔뜩 날이 선 대패로
판재를 매끄럽게 다듬어
장롱과 가재도구를 만들며
고투의 세월을 보내고

가슴속 깊이 녹아든 눈빛은
자식 위해 그늘이 되어
어둠에서 빛이 되고
언제나 손을 잡아 주셨다.

천직으로 목공일을 하며
평생을 희생해온 아버지는
강한 대팻날 연마로
야위어가는 숫돌이 되었다.

A Whetstone

My father was a carpenter.
He dropped water on his whetstone
and sharpened his blunt plane blade.
By friction, the stone made the blade sharp.

With the sharp plane
he planed away the bumps on the board
to make wardrobes and household goods.
He spent his time working hard.

Gazing lovingly at his kids,
he became a cool safe shade for them
and a bright light in the darkness;
he always held their hands.

Regarding the carpenter work as a calling,
he lived a life of dedication and sacrifice;
Sharpening the steel plane blade,
he became feeble like the weakened whetstone.

봄비

목마르던 대지는
밤새 보슬보슬 내리는 빗물을
온 몸으로 삼킨다.

가랑가랑 적시는 동안
기다림에 묻어난 여린 잎새도
연두 빛 새 옷으로 갈아입고

깊어가는 밤
창가를 적시는 빗물은
삶의 사슬에 지친 몸을 적셔
외로운 마음을 달래 주며

첫사랑이 여운을 남기듯
푸름이 스며든 싱그러움으로
생명이 꿈틀거린다.

Spring Rain

After it drizzled all night long,
the thirsty earth
swallows the rainwater.

While drizzling down,
tender leaves that waited for the rain
get dressed in their new green clothes.

On the deepening night
the rain, beating against the windows,
soothes my lonely heart,
when I'm worn-out in the chain of life.

As if first flush of love leaves an aftertaste,
a new life starts to sprout
in the green freshness of the rain.

개심사 왕벚꽃

향기어린 오월 고즈넉한
상왕산 개심사(開心寺) 대웅보전 앞
왕벚꽃이 중생을 반긴다.

아침 이슬 살포시 눈을 뜨고
법당 안에 초연히 앉아
노(老)스님의 무심한 목탁소리
숲속으로 여울지며

봄소식을 몰고 온 비비새는
멍울진 벚꽃 가지 끝을 흔들며
감미롭게 봄노래를 부르는데

끝없는 번뇌를 자르려고
흐드러지게 핀 벚꽃이
방긋 웃으며 마음을 활짝 연다.

King Cherry Blossoms
of Gaeshim Temple

In May when fragrant scents fill the air,
king cherry blossoms welcome people,
before a main hall of Gaeshim Temple at Mt. Sangwang.

Morning dewdrops softly open their eyes;
an aged monk, sitting detachedly in the hall,
is beating his wooden gong sublimely.
The beating sound resonates into the woods.

A parrot-bill bird that has brought spring news
shakes the branch of cherry blossoms,
merrily singing a sweet song.

To renounce limitless worldly desires,
cherry blossoms, in full bloom,
open up their hearts with a big smile.

제2부 · 백두대간

Part 2 · Baekdu-daegan Mountain Range

백두대간

우람한 백두산 천지에서
지리산까지 뻗어 내린 줄기
기슭마다 삶터를 열었네.

신비스러운 기암괴석 이룬
아득한 능선과 계곡들
비경이 계절의 변화 따라
정기를 받으며 사는 삶

태초에 시원의 숲속
장엄한 산줄기에 길을 열고
수많은 생명들이 오가듯

금수강산 방방곡곡에
천만년 민족의 염원을 싣고
생명이 움터 열매 맺으며
민족의 삶터에 꽃피우네.

Baekdu-daegan Mountain Range

The mountain range extends to Mt. Jiri
from Cheonji, a big crater lake of Mt. Baekdu;
every mountainside has a place of living.

The mountain ridges and valleys
of oddly-formed rocks and strangely-shaped stones
look remarkably amazing in tune with the seasons,
so their presence is a vital force.

In the beginning, the forest opened the path
leading to the great mountain range;
numerous living things have used the path.

With the ten-million-year wish of our people,
all sprout, bloom and bear fruit
all over the land of beautiful scenery;
we flourish at the core place of our people.

여름 산

한여름 뙤약볕 속에서
복잡한 회색 도시를 벗어나
방태산 자연휴양림에 들어서니
물소리가 하모니를 이루네.

자연의 흐름 속에
수정처럼 맑은 물이 반짝이고
녹수가 굽이굽이 휘감아 돌면
금방 초록으로 물들이며

꿈꾸듯 마음이 편안해져
산은 영원한 휴식처
푸르른 자연의 이치를 배우며
한세월 시원히 보내듯

폭염 속에 우거진 수목
비비새가 즐겁게 노래 부르고
두런거리며 흐르는 물소리가
세상 번뇌를 씻어 내리네.

The Summer Mountain

Under the burning sun in midsummer,
I get away from the busy gray city
and enter Mt. Bangtae that has a recreational forest,
where water flows in harmony with nature.

In the course of nature,
the pellucid water in a brook runs down.
When the water winds its way,
it is tinged with green in a moment.

It calms me down, and I feel like I'm in a dream.
A mountain is an everlasting resort,
so people learn the order of green nature,
while spending time coolly there.

In the thick woods under the burning sun,
there are parrot-bill birds singing merrily;
A brook is murmuring down through the woods,
washing away earthly agony.

송학松鶴

양재천에 두루미 한 쌍이
긴 목을 빼고
다리를 날개에 묻은 채 날아와
고고하게 춤을 춘다.

백조 발레단의 춤처럼
우아한 곡선의 몸짓으로
시작도 끝도 없이
한없이 불사르고

가슴을 휘젓고
꽃잎마다 반짝이는
보석 같은 춤사위가 들어와
내 영혼을 녹이듯

천고의 백조가
다정하게 나래 펴고
푸른 갈대 출렁이는 개천에
구름이 날듯 춤춘다.

Cranes on the Pine Tree

There are a pair of cranes at Yangjae Stream.
With their necks outstretched,
with their legs beneath their wings,
they flew here, dancing gracefully.

Like the ballet of the troupe performing 'Swan',
they make a dance movement elegantly,
by putting their passionate heart
into dancing endlessly.

Their dance is like the jewels
sparkling on every petal;
so the dance stirs my heart
and melts down my soul.

The swans, well-known from old times,
tenderly spread their wings
and dance, as if floating on clouds,
over the stream, where green reeds dance.

청송靑松

백두대간의 황장산에 뿌리내려
우뚝 서서 세월을 품고
천하를 굽어보는 소나무여!

비바람과 눈보라에 몸을 삭혀도
언제나 영롱한 초록빛을 지니고
선비처럼 꿋꿋하고 여유로워.

앙상한 가지만 남기고
엄동설한에 눈 덮일 때에는
두터운 갑옷으로 추위를 막아

옹이를 잉태하는 아픔에도
푸르름 뚝뚝 떨어지는 솔향기는
속세의 온갖 번뇌를 걷어내며

의리와 지조로
씩씩한 기개를 지닌 채
불같이 치열하게 사는 삶

긴 머리 일렁이는 구름 속에
하늘 우러러 영혼을 이야기하듯
천하를 굽어보는 소나무여!

A Green Pine Tree

O Pine Tree, you took root proudly
at Mt. Hwangjang of Baekdudaegan Mountain Range
and overlooked the world for so long.

Out of shape in rainstorms and snowstorms,
you've always been bright green,
taking a firm and good stand like a scholar.

In the frigid winter, to keep off the cold,
your leafless branches were covered with snow
as if wearing a thick leather cuirass.

Even in the pain of being gnarled with age,
you give forth a fresh scent,
easing up on the agonies in the world.

Showing a vigorous spirit
with loyalty and fidelity,
you survived in the struggle for existence.

O Pine Tree that's overlooking the world!
You seem to talk about our souls with the sky,
as your pine needles sway in the clouds.

거울 앞에서

한 세상 소망 안고 떠돌다가
온갖 괴로움 삼키며
아파하는 모습 보일 때
불효인 줄 몰랐는데

말없는 눈빛으로
모자람 깨달아 알 때까지
감탄도 나무람도 없이
너그럽게 웃으시던 모습,

속된 세상 괴로움 겪어도
못 본 듯 참으시며
눈멀고 귀 먹어
자혜롭게 사시던 어머니

어느새 검은머리 서리꽃 피고
이마에 주름살 가득한 채
움츠려든 몸, 자불(瓷佛)처럼 앉아
타다만 세월 마음 비우네.

In Front of a Mirror

I didn't know my ingratitude to my mother
until I saw my mother feeling pain
but enduring sufferings.
She ever wandered with hope in her heart.

My mother waited in silence
for me to realize my inadequacy.
Without admiration or reproach,
she just looked at me with a generous smile.

Though she experienced sufferings in the earthly world,
she pretended not to see them, by enduring them.
she lived a benevolent and smart life,
by pretending that she was blind and deaf.

In a blink, her black hair turned as white as frost flowers.
With wrinkles on her forehead, with her shriveled body,
she is seated like a porcelain Buddha statue,
as if hoping to clear her mind for the rest of her days.

청산에 올라

청옥산 계곡을 따라 오르면
가슴이 확 트이고 편안함이 들도록
포근하게 보듬어 감싸네.

산허리엔 초록빛 물들고
가슴 벅차도록 다가오는 솔향기
새롭게 마음을 깨우네.

물처럼 흘러가는 세월 속에
주렁주렁 매달린 번뇌의 시름들
깨끗이 흘려보낸 채

녹음이 우거진 여름 숲속에
즐겁게 춤추는 초록빛 숨결 돋아나
여기가 무릉도원이 아닌가.

Climbing up the Green Mountain

Climbing up through the valley of Mt. Cheong-ok
I feel openhearted and comfortable,
as the mountain embraces me.

The mountainside has a tinge of green;
the scent of pines comes to overwhelm me,
freshening up my mind.

When years flow away like water,
I let all my anguish flow away in the stream
for it to disappear completely.

In the summer forest, thick with grasses and trees,
merrily dancing green leaves smell good and fresh.
This place is Shangri-la, an exotic utopia, isn't it?

무인도

내 가슴속에 무인도가 있네
아무도 오지 않는 이곳
호젓한 오솔길에 반짝이는 별
침묵 속에 흐르는 해조음

그 곳에 가면
아무도 없지만 파도가 노래하고
사연을 고스란히 품은 채
밟지 않은 햇살이 있네.

누구에게도 손이 닿지 않은
통제할 수 있어 둘러보는 지역
적막한 밤이지만 빈 가슴으로
아무생각 없이 하늘에 안겨

간절한 욕망이 낙조 속에 묻히고
마음속에 두려움 다가오는
내 가슴 속에 푸르른 섬
아무에게도 알려지지 않는 곳...

An Uninhabited Island

My heart seems to have
an uninhabited island,
where stars twinkle over the path
and waves roll in silence.

No one is there,
but waves may sing a song.
The sunlight floods onto the place, untrodden,
by holding some stories in its heart.

The intact island is under control,
and looking around is allowed.
On the lonely night when I feel empty,
it seems the sky soothes me.

Desires are buried in the glow of the setting sun,
and I feel I shrink with fear.
However, deep in my heart,
I have an unknown green island.

채석강

변산 격포에는 고전이 쌓여있다.

책은 친구이고 지식의 보고
아득한 옛 얘기를 들려주기도 하며
미래를 예측할 수 있게 한다.

그와 아름다운 눈 맞춤은
모락모락 피어나는 책속의 언어와
상상의 노트로서 메아리친다.

책은 인생의 나침판이고
원활한 소통의 길이며 행복의 비타민
평생 편안하게 해주는 친구.

마음속에 다지는 끝없는 공감대
따뜻한 가슴속으로 미래를 엮어가는
믿음직한 동업자이다.

The Chaeseok River

Classic books seem to be piled up at Gyeokpo, Byeonsan.

A book is a friend and a storehouse of knowledge.
So it tells us great old-time stories,
making us predict the future.

When we practice eye contact with it,
good words come out of it
echoing in our imagination.

A book is a compass for our life,
a way of smooth communication, and vitamins for happiness.
It's also a life-long friend, making us feel comfortable.

With a bond of infinite sympathy developed in our hearts,
it shapes our heart-warming future;
hence, it must be our reliable partner.

대청마루

고향집 마루는 암홍색으로 빛난다.

바닥을 걸레로 닦고 또 닦아
듬성듬성 옹이 박힌 소나무 무늬 결에
지나온 집안의 내력들이 스며들어
질항아리처럼 반짝인다.

우주를 제 몸에 담은 나무들
그 목리(木理)에 꿰맞추어진 마루널판
가지런한 질서로 깔려 향기피우고
추울 때엔 군불에 뎁혀지고

인생의 주춧돌이 되어
나이테를 더해가는 아련한 추억 속에
뜨거운 가슴속에 사무치는 마음
흑백사진으로만 남아있다.

험난한 인생살이 버거울 때
눈을 감고 명상하듯 앉아있으면
긴 세월 흘러도 두고 온 고향마루 생각
잊을 수 없어 눈물이 앞선다.

The Wood-floored Main Hall

The wooden floor of my hometown has a shiny dark-red color.

When wiped a lot with a damp cloth,
the floor shines brightly like a glossy crock.
The history of my family seems to run onto the floor
of the pine boards that are sparsely gnarled.

Each plank of wood contains the universe;
so, boarding the floor, people used the grain of wood.
The neatly arranged boards gave forth pleasant scents;
when it was cold, people heated the wooden floor warm.

The floor has been a cornerstone of my life;
as years flow on, my memory is hazy and vague.
But the memory of the floor still lingers in my heart,
like a bland-and-white photo.

When life is so hard
I sit with my eyes closed, as if doing meditation.
Years and years went by, but I think of the wooden floor;
I cannot recall it without tears.

추회追懷

길지도 않은 우리 인생
고민하지 말고 서로의 고통을 나누며
흘러가는 강물처럼 바위를 만나면 돌아가고
웅덩이를 만나면 고여 있다가
행복을 이루어가면서 살아가리.

사랑하며 살아도 너무 짧은 삶
주고 또 베풀어도 남는 것들인데
웬 욕심으로 무거운 짐을 지고
마음의 문을 굳게 닫고
서로 싸우면서 상처만 남기는가.

그대 걸어온 길 되돌아보면
저려오는 아픈 통증 때문에
긴 한숨 내쉬기보다 순간순간 설레게 했던
행복한 기억들로 환한 미소 머금은 채
호탕한 모습 보이던 때도 있었지 않았나.

Retrospection

Our life is not as long as we think,
so I'll not worry; I'll share pain with others.
Like a river, I'll turn around, when I face a huge rock.
When I meet a pool of water, I'll linger in the pool.
Making happiness in it, I'll lead a life.

Though I live with love, life is too short.
I've been beneficent to others, but there's still a lot left.
If I shut the door of my heart and fight against others,
struggling under a heavy load of greed,
it'll leave scars to me and others.

When I look back on each path I have taken so far,
compassion tugs at my heart.
I won't draw a long sigh; with such happy memories
as sweet heart-throbbing moments,
I once showed others that I'm a broad-minded person.

무궁화동산

산 좋고 물 맑은 한반도에
꽃잎마다 새겨진 아픔 달래주는
사랑스런 그 이름 무궁화

나라를 상징하는 국화로
흰색의 꽃잎에 화심(花心)깊숙이
붉은 색 자리 잡은 단심(丹心)으로
태양과 운명을 같이하는 꽃

무궁한 태극혼의 정신 이어받아
영원무궁토록 이 땅에 곱게 누려갈
하늘백성인 한민족의 얼

맑고 환한 옷차림으로
안으로 움츠렸던 가슴 활짝 펴고
하늘높이 우러러 웃음꽃 피워

수없이 많은 세월 변한다 해도
삼천리 금수강산 방방곡곡 물들여
영원한 민족 번영을 이루리.

The Land of Rose-of-Sharon

On the Korean peninsula of good mountains and waters,
the lovely flowers, Rose-of-Sharon, burst into blossom;
the flower's name alleviates the pain of each petal.

The flower is our national flower, a symbol of our nation.
Showing the red sincere heart
at the base of each white petal,
the flower has shared its destiny with the sun.

As the people closest to heaven,
we'll succeed to the spirit of the great ultimate,
making it bloom and flourish on this land forever.

Dressed in neat and bright clothes,
we'll straighten ourselves up, not cowering,
and smile brightly towards the sky.

Though many years pass and times change,
the beautiful land of Korea, far and wide,
will prosper and flourish forever.

물안개

여명이 터오는 아침
옥정호 위로 자욱이 떠오르는
물안개로 내 마음 황홀해진다.

화려한 무도회가 열리듯
아련한 모습으로 너울너울 춤추며
솜털같이 떠오르는 물보라

손끝에 너울거리는 하얀 빛
밤새 삭히지 못한 응어리 한 줌
나래 치며 춤추는 것일까.

춤사위가 끝난 이 시간에도
잊지 못할 한 조각의 추억으로
기억 속에 아련히 피어오른다.

A Dense Mist

At daybreak, early in the morning
a dense mist lies over Okjeong Lake,
which makes me ecstatic about the beauty.

As if giving a splendid dance party,
a spray of water is fanning up into the air,
dimly undulating over the lake.

A white light is wavering over my extended fingers.
Not removing its discontent all night long,
is it now dancing, like flapping the wings?

When the dancing is over,
the mist, as an unforgettable reminiscence,
is rising, shimmering in the memory.

빗소리

소낙비가 내리는 날
쏟아지는 빗줄기가 창가로 낙하하며
박자를 맞추어 노래한다.

어린 시절 학교 가던 길
빗물이 갑자기 불어나 죽마고우들과 함께
손에 손잡고 개울을 건너던 기억 들...

악보와 악기가 없어도
뚜두둑 뚜두둑 떨어지는 빗소리와 함께
가슴속에 강물이 흘러 합창하듯

밤새 내리는 비가 환상곡이 되고
망망한 바다는 쉼 없이 일렁이며 춤추듯
바다의 교향곡이 되었다.

The Sound of Rain

When heavy rain splatters,
rain, falling down by the window,
sings to the beat.

When I was young, on the way to school,
the stream suddenly rose because of the heavy rain;
hand in hand with my friends, I crossed the stream.

With no music scores and musical instruments,
the rain sings, falling pitter-patter on the ground.
In my heart, a river sounds like singing in chorus.

The rain, falling all night, becomes fantasia;
the open sea, restlessly pitching and rolling,
becomes symphony.

쑥

뿌리에 숨긴 기질은
어둠을 비집고 일어서
새봄을 향긋하게 장식하네.

초토화된 흙더미 속에서도
갈기갈기 찢기고 잘린 채
끈질기게 일어서며

암울했던 시대에
민초들의 갖은 핍박으로
뼈를 깎는 절망의 고통 감내하듯

칠흑의 어둠을 안고
강인한 생명력으로 깨어나
굳세게 일어서네.

Mugwort

Its temperamental trait, hidden in the roots,
comes out of the darkness,
decorating new spring with its fragrance.

Though ripped up and cut down
in the desolated land,
it struggled to be up perseveringly.

Enduring excruciating pain
during the dark years,
it survived through people's persecution.

Embracing the pitch darkness,
it wakes up with strong vitality
and stands up undauntedly.

질경이

길섶에 뿌리내려
짓밟히고 찢겨 버림받아도
온몸으로 참고 견디며 일어선다.

타는 목마름에
살을 맞대고 살아가는
민초들의 처절한 고통의 시간들

풀벌레 우는 칠흑의 밤
어둠 뚫고 치열하게 싹을 틔워
잃어버린 꿈을 찾으려 한다.

야멸찬 구둣발에 짓밟히며
줄기가 부스러지고 으깨어져
혼신을 추스르지 못할 지라도

척박한 땅에 돋아나는 뿌리들은
끈질기게 목숨 걸고 돋아나
절망의 그늘에서 부활한나.

Plantains

As plantains take roots by a roadside,
they can be trampled, torn, or deserted.
But they endure the trial to stand up.

Feeling the burning thirst,
the grass roots live, tangled up together,
and survive horrible sufferings.

On a pitch-dark night when grass bugs chirp,
the grass roots struggle to sprout in the darkness,
searching for their lost dreams.

Trampled by cold-hearted pedestrians,
the stems are too broken and crushed
to revive their bodies and souls.

The roots sprouting even in barren soil
are tenacious of life,
so they revive in the shadow of despair.

제3부 · 먼 산
Part 3 · A Distant Mountain

먼 산

구름을 벗어난 먼 산은
참선하여 해탈하려는 고승처럼
초연히 좌선을 하는 중이라네

고요 속에 침묵하며
법열(法悅)의 깊은 이치를 깨달아
도량이 넓고 맑게 일깨우는 듯

누구에게나 열려진 공간
스며든 해를 가슴에 안은 채
목마른 이에게 감로수가 되고

아픔의 세월 번뇌에 찌든 육신처럼
영혼의 꽃잎 피울 수 있도록
언제나 유유자적하는 걸

멀리 있어도 누구에게나
너그럽고 자혜로움 가득히
묵언수행(黙言修行)중이라네

A Distant Mountain

Getting out of the clouds,
a distant mountain does Zen meditation
like a Buddhist monk who wants to reach Nirvana.

Keeping silent in a great stillness,
it seems to realize the deep meaning of religious ecstasy
and awaken a broad and clear attitude.

The mountain is the place open to anyone;
though holding the sun tight to its chest,
it can be like sweet water to those who are thirsty.

As if our bodies, suffering from long agony,
can have petals for the souls,
the mountain always keeps peaceful.

Though it is far away, to anyone
it is generous and benevolent,
meditating silently.

영겁永劫의 강

비단자락 굽이굽이 흐르며
꽃구름 수놓고 정겹게 살아온 물줄기
제 몸을 낮추며 깊어만 간다.

험난한 산굽이를 넘을 때
외롭고 힘겹지만 잠시 쉬어가는 곳에
끼리끼리 푸르른 피를 나누고

문명이 토해낸
도시의 오물들을 머금고도
온 누리를 골고루 촉촉하게 적시고
물줄기를 흐르게 한다.

사려 깊게 제 갈길 가며
이 땅을 밟고 살아온
온유한 사람들의 혼이 서린
역사의 숨겨진 자취들…

억만년 태고의 이야기들
고을마다 지나온 긴긴 자취 보여주며
후손들에게 좋은 꿈을 전한다.

The Eternal River

Glittering like silk, the river meanders along;
with glowing clouds on its surface, it flows affectionately.
Lying low, it is getting deeper.

Flowing along a bend of a rough mountain,
the river looks lonely and tired.
Taking a short rest, it shares fresh green with others.

Though it holds some urban rubbish and filth
that civilization has brought,
the river flows with a lively current,
making the world moist equally.

The river embraces the hidden history
about the souls of the meek people
who have gone their respective ways
considerately on this land...

Telling the stories of high antiquity,
showing the traces of its visit to each village,
it conveys hopes and dreams to our descendants.

풍향

가끔은 나도 모르게
꿈을 꾸듯 당신의 집 앞을
하염없이 서성거렸네.

창 너머로 새어나오는
불빛조차 눈이 부시어
더욱 초라해지고

안락한 잠자리에서
감미로운 분위기를
즐기고 있을지 모르는데

식지 않는 무거운 정념을
사랑으로 물들인
핑크빛 물감인 걸

내 마음 흔들어
눈짓 한번 주지 않고 모른척한
매정한 당신이지만

먼 훗날 삶 끝날 때 까지
그대 향해 변치 않고
사모하는 마음 영원하리.

The Direction of the Wind

Sometimes I paced up and down
blankly in spite of myself
in front of your house as if in reverie.

When a thread of light emerged from your window,
even the light was too bright for my eyes,
and I really felt miserable.

However, I guessed you were
on your comfy bed,
enjoying a mellow mood.

My burning love toward you
will be never gone at all;
instead, it still has a tinge of pink.

You put me in complete turmoil,
but you haven't even looked at me.
How heartless you are!

Even so, until the end of my life,
I will maintain a steadfast love for you;
my love will last forever.

열반涅槃

생이란 한 조각 뜬구름
숨 한번 들여 마시고
마신 숨 다시 토해내면
그게 살아있다는 증표

절개된 목어(木魚) 등의
각인된 목탁소리에
다갈색 연록 출렁거리네.

우담바라처럼 시어(詩語)가 들면
좋은 시 한편 지어
즈믄 밤 열반에 들고
죽어서도 영원히 살려네.

Nirvana

Life is a speck of cloud;
breathing in
and then breathing out
means I am alive.

To the sound of a fish-shaped wooden clapper
that has small incisions on it,
brown-tinted greenery is swaying.

When poetic words come to me like Udambara*,
I will write a good poem;
and, at night when I enter Nirvana,
the poem will make me live forever.

* Udambara: a Sanskrit word, meaning 'a mysterious and miraculous flower'

인연

떠나려 할 때 보내주고
높이 날아가려 할 때
풀어주고 당기는 줄

설레는 마음으로
한 평생 곁에 머무르려 했으나
바람을 선택한 그대,

줄을 잘라
죽음에 입 맞추며
나뭇가지에 찢기고 떨어진
빗나간 인생의 슬픈 운명,

이제 모든 것 다 주려해도
돌아오지 못하는 그 사람
낙엽처럼 가슴에 쌓이네.

A Fateful Relationship

I let her go, as she wanted to leave;
I loosened the rope, sometimes giving a pull,
as she wanted to fly high.

In excitement
I wanted to stay with her all my life,
but she chose a wind.

Cutting the rope
she kissed death;
what a sad fate for the stray life,
as it was torn by a bough and fell off.

Now I want to give her everything,
but she cannot come back to me;
only longing is piled up like fallen leaves.

세월의 흔적

인생길은 세월의 틈바퀴에서
오고 가는지도 모른 채 스스로 원망하며
세월 흘러간 빈자리를 잊고 살았네.

'86 아시안게임과 '88 서울올림픽에
전기설비의 안전대책을 맡아 정전 없는
전기를 공급하며 대회를 성공으로
이끌어 가도록 하였다는 걸

반평생을 넘어서 생각하니
가슴에 꽃향기 피어들고 생의 보람으로
남아 있다는 걸 훗날 알게 되었네.

세월이 흘러간 후에도 가슴에
서울올림픽 성화가 온 누리에 타올랐던
그리운 추억의 흔적으로 남아있네.

The Trace of Time

Living a very full and hectic life,
I didn't know the years came and went;
I blame myself, for I forgot the years roll by.

I was in charge of the electrical safety
for the '86 Asian Games and the '88 Seoul Olympic Games.
I contributed to the success of the two Games,
by supplying electricity, not causing a blackout.

After spending half my life, I look back on it.
The scent of the flowers still wafts into my heart,
and now I realize I've lived a fruitful life.

Decades later, in my heart,
the Seoul Olympic torch still blazes up
to light the world, as the good trace of time.

억새꽃 향연

늦가을 억새 숲에 가면
저만치서 흔들어대는 솔바람이
내 마음 속에 불을 지핀다.

군악대가 사열하고
오케스트라의 합주곡이 울리면
백조는 군무를 곱게 춘다.

정녕 어떠한 향연도
석양에 반짝이는 은빛 물결을
상상해 볼 수도 없는데

능선에서 백발의 신선이
삶에 지친 몸을 포근히 감싸며
해묵은 번뇌를 씻어 준다.

Silver Grass Festival

On a silver grass field in late fall,
a cool breeze blows in the distance,
starting a fire in my soul.

On the field, an army band seems to be lined up;
along with an orchestra performance,
white swans seem to dance in group.

It may be impossible for other festivals
to have the silver ripples
sparkling in the evening sun.

I feel a gray-haired mountain god
hugging my exhausted body warmly
and removing my anguish of life.

행복한 동행

끈끈하게 맺어진 인연으로
모닥불을 피운 듯 따뜻한 동행 길은
고통이 따르지만 행복합니다.

담소로 밀어를 나누며
향기 그윽한 꽃길을 함께 걷는 동안
마음이 하늘빛처럼 맑아지고

은은한 국화향기가 스미는
꽃길을 걸으며 한결같은 삶속에서
불꽃같이 활활 타오르듯이

강물같이 흘러 흘러가는 세월
폭풍우가 몰아쳐도 서로 끌어안고
마지막 순간까지 사랑하기를…

Happy Together

Going together by creating a close relationship.
As if making a bonfire, it is awesome,
though there may be some troubles.

Having a friendly talk with each other,
we walk together along a path of fragrant flowers;
then our minds are as clear as a sky.

Walking along the path of fragrant chrysanthemums,
we feel like a flame can blaze fervidly,
even in our unchanging lives.

Years that flow on like rivers;
even in severe storms, we'll hug each other,
loving each other to the last moment.

단풍

늦가을 설악산에 오르면
맑은 하늘아래 물감을 풀어놓은 듯
꿈이 가득 찬 나무들을 본다.

자연은 추억을 잉태하고
만산(滿山)이 굽이굽이 홍엽으로
열정에 취해 불꽃을 지피는데

가을 끝자락 붉은 산은
누구에게나 피를 빠르게 돌게 하며
인정 많은 시인이 되게 한다.

사람이 살면서 한 순간이라도
단풍처럼 울긋불긋 타오를 수 있다면
후회 없는 삶이 될 텐데

한세상 초록으로 살아가다가
마지막 떠날 때를 알고 몸을 낮추며
낙엽 되어 깊은 잠에 빠진다.

Autumn Foliage

Climbing up Mt. Seorak in late autumn,
I see trees filled with dreams;
O the hues of the foliage under the clear blue sky.

Nature gives birth to memories;
the whole mountain is ablaze with red foliage
along its winding valleys and mountainside.

The sight of red mountains, at the end of autumn,
causes our blood to circulate faster,
making us become warm-hearted poets.

If we can be ablaze with glaring colors
even for a moment in our life,
we'll have a life without regrets.

I have lived a full life so far;
As I know when I finally leave, I lie low,
like a fallen leaf, and fall into a deep sleep.

바람 속에서

나의 길에는 항상 바람이 분다.
가지 많은 나무에 바람 잘 날 없듯이
우환과 근심이 그칠 새 없다.

이른 새벽 별을 바라보려고
창을 열면 시린 가슴에
쓸쓸한 바람이 안기어 온다.

언 땅 녹여 싹을 틔울 때나
초록 들판을 황금빛으로 물들일 때도
바람 속에 바람을 품고 있듯이

외롭고 공허한 날에
하늘이 온 세상을 흔들어 놓을 때도
심연 위에 경멸(輕蔑)을 뿌린다.

In the Wind

It is always windy on my way.
As if trees with lots of branches catch much wind,
I constantly suffer from troubles and anxieties.

When I open a window
to look up at stars at early dawn,
a lonely wind nestles in my broken heart.

When thawing the frozen ground to shoot out buds,
when turning the green fields to golden fields,
a wind seems to hold another wind in its arms.

When I feel lonely or empty,
when the sky shakes the whole world,
the winds seem to pour scorn on the abyss.

구름의 집

하늘에 펼쳐놓은 화폭이다.

구름은 무한 공간을
아름답게 수놓으며 곡예 하듯
산천을 벗 삼아 유유히 흘러간다.

뭉게구름 솜처럼 흘러와
지상에 떠도는 은유를 끌어 올려
꿈처럼 곱게 펼쳐 놓는다.

어디서 만들어져 어디로 가는가.
하늘에 집을 짓고 온갖 사연 풀어
덧없이 살아지는 인생이듯

서창에 드리우는 저녁노을
덧없는 자취들마다 순수하고
맑은 넋 꿈길처럼 황홀하다.

The House of Clouds

The picturesque scenery of the sky.

Clouds drift leisurely in infinite space,
as if embroidering with great dexterity,
in the companionship of hills and streams.

White fluffy clouds float like soft cotton,
pulling up the poetic images of the ground,
and spreading them beautifully in the air.

Where were they made and where are they going?
They built a house in the sky and now talk a lot,
as if telling that life is transient.

A westward window is dyed red by the sunset.
Each transient trace has purity;
like in a dream, the pure spirit feels ecstasy.

바람의 시

대지 위 부는 바람은 방랑 시인.

대나무 숲을 지나가며
고요에 얽혔던 하늘의 적막을 깨는 듯
멋과 풍요를 함유한 아름다운 소리로
볼을 비비듯 스치며 시를 읊조린다.

때로는 소프라노 음색을 지닌
암벽을 지나는 빠르고 강한 기교로
훗날 마주할 기약 없이 초조감을 감추지 못하며
경쾌하게 시(詩)노래를 부르며 떠난다.

비자 없이도 천하를 여기저기
주유(周遊)하고 장기 체류하거나 입주한 적이 없는
산과 들을 기숙사로 여기며
떠돌이처럼 다니는 바람이듯

후미진 곳 닫힌 문을 두드리며
목이 쉬도록 진한 울음으로 시를 읊조리며
강 언덕 미끄러지듯 타는 노을을 마시며
파도를 타고 흔적 없이 강 건너 가는가.

The Poem of the Wind

The wind blowing over the ground is a wandering poet.

Passing by a bamboo grove,
the wind sounds like breaking the silence of the sky.
With the awesome sound of greatness and richness,
the wind, as if rubbing cheeks, recites a poem,

Sometimes singing in soprano,
the wind fast passes by a huge rock with a technique.
Impatiently without a promise to meet again,
it leaves, swingingly singing poetic songs.

Going around the world without a visa,
the wind travels or stays for a long time.
Thinking of all the hills and fields as its house,
it roams there, whistling through them.

Knocking on the closed doors at a secluded spot,
the wind shouts itself hoarse, reciting a poem.
As if sliding down the bank of a river at sunset,
does it ride the waves, crossing the river with no trace?

그리운 밤에

침묵을 톱질하는
귀뚜라미 소리에 가을이 흐르며
잠 못 이루는 밤 기억 속에
살아오는 해맑은 얼굴.

추억으로 묻어오는 고운 목소리
속삭이듯 차오르고
못 견디게 그리워 떠도는 허공 속
불러보는 그 이름.

잃어버린 시간 속에
수없이 되새겨도 가시지 않는 갈증
얼룩진 흔적 씻어내어 그대 있는 곳
내 마음 보내 드리리.

Missing You at Night

The crickets, chirping loudly,
break silence on an autumn night.
And your bright face comes into my mind,
making me sleepless.

Your sweet voice, lingering in my memory,
seems to whisper to me now.
As I cannot refrain from missing you,
I call your name into the air.

I ruminate of lost time a great deal,
but I only have an unquenchable thirst.
After washing some bad stains out,
I'll send my heart to your place.

신호등

숨 가쁘게 돌아가는 세상
걸어가야 하는 미지의 길을 위해서
언제나 신호등을 지켜보네.

신호등은 빨간불을 켜다가도
시간이 흐르면 다시 파란불이 켜져
멈춰 있는 길을 가도록 하며

사람이 계속 쉬지 않도록
파란불과 빨간불이 조화를 이루며
걷다 잠시 쉬고 반복해 걷듯

절망하여 뒤돌아서지 않는 한
마지막 종착역에 도달한다는 사실
바로 그게 인생길이 아닌가.

Traffic Lights

The world is coming thick and fast.
To go on the untraveled road,
I always see traffic lights.

Though the light is red now,
it turns green over time
for pedestrians to keep going.

In order for people not to stop long,
the lights turn green or red in harmony,
so people walk, take a short rest, and walk again.

If they don't turn around in despair,
at last they'll reach the final destination.
Isn't it similar to the path of life?

가을이 오면

가을 산과 들은
해맑은 햇살을 베어 담아
화려한 옷으로 단장한다.

여름 내내 푸르던 잎사귀
핏빛으로 달아오른 해를 삼켜
울긋불긋 색색으로 물들고

옷깃에 묻어 떠는 저녁 햇살
티 없이 맑은 눈에 젖어
고요히 잠긴다.

산과 들이 붉게 익어 가듯
가슴까지 발그레하게 물들어
짙은 그리움을 남겨둔 채

햇살이 어둠 속으로 지는 순간
노을빛으로 빨려드는 단풍
절정의 설움에 눈이 부시다.

When Autumn Comes

Autumn mountains and fields
get decorated with flash clothes,
by mingling with bright sunshine.

The leaves that were green all summer
swallow a blood-red hot sun
and then turn red and yellow.

Lingering on your lapel,
the evening sunlight is silently absorbed
into your flawless clear eyes.

Mountains and fields turn red,
and even my heart is tinged with red,
leaving a deep longing behind.

At the moment the sunlight falls into the darkness
autumn colors are sucked into the sunset.
The sad color on the peak is so dazzling.

제4부 · 인생의 길목에서

Part 4 · On the Corner of My Life

인생의 길목에서

텅 빈 바랑에 바람을 담아
무거운 시간의 그림자를 데리고
아름다운 꿈을 찾아
쉼 없이 한 발짝씩 걸어왔다.

돌아보면 모두 걷고 싶어 하던
수많은 갈래 길이 있지만
각자 걸어가는 길은 하나

곧은길만 잇따라 가는 줄 알지만
앞서거니 뒤서거니 하며
지친 새벽길

숨차게 지나가고
험한 협곡의 고난의 길도
스스로 갈고 닦으며 가야하는 걸

빈 바랑 속에 하나둘 채워지는
영혼의 맑은 양식들
한 순간 깨우침의 향기 마시며
오늘도 미로를 걷는다.

On the Corner of My Life

Putting only a wind in my empty knapsack,
I walked step by step without a break
even in times of pressure or hardship,
to search for a beautiful dream.

There were lots of roads, back then,
which we all wanted to walk on,
but each of us had to take only one road.

I didn't follow only a direct route;
instead, I raced neck and neck with others
on a curved road, until I got tired around dawn.

While running out of breath,
I also faced a road as awful as a ravine,
but I went forward, by cultivating myself.

My knapsack that was empty
was filled with spiritual food, bit by bit.
Wishing for a moment of enlightenment,
I still walk in the maze today, too.

호반의 찻집

그리움이 쌓일 때면
눈길을 걷던 호숫가 찻집에서
그녀와 함께 커피를 마시네.

조용히 흐르는 음율 속에
어우러진 향내음 새겨 마시면
어느새 커피 잔은 비워져
공허한 마음 갈증으로 남고

소리 없이 내리는 함박눈이
그때 그날처럼 포근하게
발자국을 지울 무렵엔

가로등 불빛이 반짝이며
향그러운 한 잔의 커피 내음처럼
애정 어린 추억 젖어오네.

The Cafe by the Lake

When I feel lots of longing,
I imagine I'm with her, having coffee at the cafe
by the lake, where we once stepped on snow.

Listening to soft music,
I have coffee, captivated by the flavor.
In a blink, my cup is empty,
and I feel empty with a thirst for love.

Big snowflakes, quietly falling down,
cover footprints as snugly
as snow did then.

When the street lights glow,
I indulge in reminiscence
like I do so by coffee flavor.

바다의 언어

바다는 파도로 언어를 구사한다.

넓고 아득한 수평선에서
밀려오는 세찬 파도는
상형문자로 소리를 전한다.

끊임없이 돌진하는 파도는
출렁이고 찢기며 부서져
죽음과 부활을 거듭 반복하며
영원히 언어의 씨앗을 뿌린다.

출렁이는 파도의 음운(音韻),
썰물과 밀물의 음직임에서
율조(律調)의 변화를 보이고
물방울의 진동으로 파도가 되어
언어로 전하듯

고음과 저음 때로는 은은하게
시를 읊조리고 노래 부르며
망설임 없이 언어를 구사한다.

The Language of the Sea

The sea talks, by using waves.

From the far horizon of the open sea,
rough waves surge ceaselessly,
conveying the sound with pictograph signs.

The surging waves never stop,
but roll, split and break.
Repeating the cycle of death and rebirth,
the waves perpetually sow the seeds of language.

The sounds of curling waves
and the ebb and flow of the sea
change the tone of waves.
By the vibration of water drops, waves rise
as if conveying it in their language.

In high or low tones, sometimes in deep tones,
the waves recite poems and sing songs,
not hesitating to speak their language.

바다시집

해변 모래밭에 시를 써놓으면
파도가 덮쳐 소멸 되는가 했더니
곧 부활하여 시를 읊조린다.

제방과 부두, 바위섬에서도
철썩여 망망대해로 번지고
적을 수 없는 활자로 바다에 시를 쓰며
형형색색 밀려 퍼진다.

파도는 눈이 부시고 시릴 때
잠시 눈을 감고 있다가 풀리는 듯하면
다시 시를 읊조리고 춤을 추며
해류를 따라 넓고 멀리 번진다.

삶속에 저며 오는 바람으로
새벽 바다를 흔드는 빛과 물 조화롭게
거친 세월의 자국마다
흥겨운 시노래를 연주한다.

The Collection of Poems by the Sea

If I write a poem on a beach,
waves attack to remove it.
But soon the poem is revived and recited.

Splashing against a dike, a dock, and a rocky isle,
my poem is carried to the open sea.
Waves roll out colorfully, writing a poem on the sea,
where it's impossible to be written in type.

Feeling dazzled by sparkling lights,
waves close their eyes for a moment;
when they feel ok, they recite the poem again,
dancing and moving along the currents.

Though facing the piercing winds,
waves are in tune with early morning sunlight and water;
whenever having a rough time,
waves play poetic songs in a merry tune.

겨울 소나타

바람이 빗질하는 하늘
진통 끝에 순산한 달덩이가
새털구름을 다리미질한다.

마음이 둥둥 떠다니는
어두컴컴한 산골마을에
별이 반짝이며 쏟아져 내리고

문명의 불빛들은
하늘의 별들과 교신하는 듯
공중으로 빛살을 퍼트려

산야의 침묵을 깨우느라
우거진 숲 넉넉한 어깨위로
교향곡을 깔아 놓는가?

변화무쌍한 선율이
지상에서 천상으로 흐르며
끝없이 울려 퍼진다.

Winter Sonata

The wind sweeps the sky;
A round moon, coming out after much pain,
presses cirrus clouds to be in good shape.

In a dark mountain village,
where I feel I'm so high up,
lights of twinkling stars pour down.

The lights in our civilized societies
seem to communicate with the twinkling stars,
by shooting up into the air.

Wanting to break the silence of hills and fields,
are the lights playing a symphony
over the dense woods?

Drifting from the ground to the sky,
a melody, ever-changing,
resonates endlessly.

촛불

어둠 밀어내는 그대에게
다가가면 갈수록
포근하게 감싸주네요.

스스로 아픔을 먹고
밤마다 촉촉이 적셔주는
가슴 아픈 당신은
어떻게 견디시나요.

나를 밝혀주는
그 붉은 꽃 은은히 타올라
샘솟듯 솟아오르네요.

Candlelight

You push away darkness;
the closer I get to you
the more warmly you embrace me.

Eating up your agony,
you soothe me every night;
you look brokenhearted,
but how do you endure it?

You shed light on me;
the red flame flickers weakly and then soars up
as if water gushes out of the spring.

마음의 창

하늘은 바라보는 거울
저마다 사람들의 마음속에는
자신을 보는 창이 있네.

하늘빛 창을 열면
소리 없이 찾아온 그리움 가득
당신이 주는 고마운 꽃잎.

그 속에 간절한 소망과
애틋한 사랑, 오래 간직한 행복
마음까지도 들어있듯

인생의 잊을 수 없는 여운
창이 열리면 성숙한 사랑으로
창문도 노을로 꽃피리.

The Window of the Mind

The sky is a mirror we look in.
People have, in their minds, their own windows,
through which they see themselves.

When I open the sky-blue window
I see your good petals of deep longing
that visits me silently.

In the petals, there seem to be your earnest wish,
your ardent love, your long-held happiness,
and even your tender heart.

The unforgettable emotion still lingers in my life;
when the window is open, it'll blaze red
by my love that is fully ripe.

조선 소나무

수천 년 풍상을 겪으며
혹독한 설한(雪寒)과 폭풍에도
꿋꿋한 기개로 살아온 소나무

무참히도 짓밟혀
기울던 사직을 곧추 세우기 위해
고초를 얼마나 겪어야했던가.

일제 치하에 온 몸을
갈기갈기 찢기고 부서지며
거친 억압에도 견뎌 내듯

강인한 생명력으로
흔들면 흔들수록 뿌리 깊게 내려
무궁하게 살아 숨 쉬네.

Joseon Pine Trees

Suffering hardships over millennia
in severe cold snowing weather and tempests,
the pine trees survived with a strong spirit.

When they were brutally trampled,
how much did the people suffer hardships
to save their country from collapsing?

Under Japanese imperialism
the people, torn to pieces,
endured the harsh restraint.

With a strong and vibrant life force,
the pine trees became immortal,
by taking roots deeper even when they were shaken.

물이 흐르듯

낮은 곳으로 물이 흐르듯
투명하게 휘돌아 가
목마른 자에게 생명수 주리.

찌들어 남루한 잔해들을
깨끗이 씻어 내리며
점점 낮은 곳으로 임하리.

한없이 흐르다 바다에 모여
물의 생리에 맞게
삶을 뒤돌아보며 살아가리.

Just As Water Flows

Water tends to flow downward;
it weaves its way transparently,
giving life-giving water to thirsty men.

Clearing away the debris
that's old and feculent,
it will flow to a lower place.

It flows on and on, up to a sea;
according to the physiology of water,
it'll stay there, looking back at the past years.

인동초

먹구름 휘몰아치는 눈보라에
불굴의 의지로 온몸을 던져
시련을 이겨내며 살아가네.

아픔을 겪으면서도
고난과 역경이 끝없이 이어졌지만
하늘의 서기를 받아 안고 긴긴 날
꽃을 잉태하여 활짝 피었네.

마땅히 가야하는 길
향락도 아니고 슬픔도 아니며
저마다 오늘보다 나아지도록
진력하는 게 인생이라고

세찬 눈보라에 꺾이지 않고
시련 속에 맑은 햇살 영원히
꽃을 피워 은은히 향기 피우네.

Honeysuckle

In the midst of a raging blizzard,
the honeysuckle of an indomitable will
overcame ordeals and goes on with its life.

Having suffered pain
in so many adversities and hardships,
the honeysuckle has blossomed
with energy raining down from the sky.

What I have to take
is neither enjoyment nor sadness;
actually life means
trying to be better than today.

Honeysuckle wasn't beaten by a blizzard,
but found sunlight even in the adversity;
it has blossomed, shedding their fragrance around.

향수鄕愁

봄이 되면 버들가지 춤을 추고
실개천엔 졸졸졸 흐르는 시냇물이
흥겹게 노래를 부르며 흘렀네.

들판을 수놓는 냉이며 달래는
아낙들의 손길 따라 봄 향기 그윽한데
동화처럼 떠오르는 그리운 산천

즐거워 언제나 모이던 곳
웃는 소리와 노랫소리 들려오고
파란 물결치는 황금 들녘에서

선동(善童)들의 정겨운 노랫소리
어두움 속에서 별들을 보며
이슬 머금고 꽃피는 금성마을.

Nostalgia

In springtime, the branches of a willow tree danced;
the water rippling in a streamlet
flowed down, singing merrily.

On the fields, there are shepherd's purse and wild chive
giving forth an odor of spring when women pick them.
I recall the scenery of my hometown, like that of fairy-tales.

Where people always gathered in amusement,
I heard them laugh and sing together.
The wind rippled green grass in the golden fields.

Good little boys sang affectionate songs,
looking up at the stars in pitch darkness;
in Geumseong Village, flowers bloomed, wet with dew.

비천飛天

죽어 하늘나라로 가는 길
오직 한 길뿐인 운명의 길이 되어
순간순간 생각을 떨쳐버리고
자신도 모르게 날아간다.

먼 길 이정표, 길잡이도 없이
싫어도 본향으로 돌아가야 할 길
웃을 수 있는 내일을 소망으로
홀로 미련 없이 떠나야 할 텐데

살면서 얻는 온갖 것 남겨두고
길동무 없이 삼베옷 한 벌 걸치고
하늘로 영혼의 날개를 달고
혼자서 쓸쓸히 가야만 하는가.

어차피 가야할 길이라면
인생길 거룩하게 마무리하고
하늘에 떠있는 별이 있는 곳으로
후회 없이 구름 따라 떠나가리.

Flying to Heaven

The way to heaven, after death;
we all are destined to go the way.
But each moment, shaking off the thought,
we fly there in spite of ourselves.

A long way with no road signs and no guides.
Alas, the way to go back to my original home.
Hoping for tomorrow I can smile,
I wish to leave alone without regrets.

Leaving all the things that I've got in my life,
I should go in hemp clothes with no fellow travelers.
Do I have to go to heaven alone in loneliness,
with my soul wings opened up ?

If it is the way I should go
I'll end my days divinely.
Then, following clouds without any regrets,
I'll go to heaven, the world of stars.

화롯불

할아버지는 화롯불이셨네.

엄동설한을 지나기 위하여
숯불 가득 담아 방 한가운데 모셔
추위를 녹여주는 불씨이셨네.

숯 검댕이 속을 태워
손자들의 시린 가슴 다독여주던
할아버지는 따뜻한 사랑이셨네.

유난히 흰 수염이 많으시고
엄하면서 자애로움이 넘쳐
인자하신 할아버지셨네.

The Brazier's Flame

My grandfather was like a brazier's flame.

All through the cold winter months,
his brazier, filled with burning charcoals, was put
in the center of a room to melt the cold away.

Burning the black charcoals,
he used to comfort his grandsons
with his warm and sweet love.

He wore a heavy beard and mustache.
Though he was quite strict,
he was a man with a benevolent heart.

굽은 소나무

깎아지른 산마루턱에서
빈 마음으로 하늘을 바라보며
푸른빛 잃지 않고 향기를 뿜어낸다.

굽은 소나무 선산 지키듯이
비가 쏟아지고 바람 불며
눈보라가 세차게 휘몰아쳐도
지조를 지키며 살아온 삶

파고드는 그리움 안고
이제 새우등처럼 허리가 굽어
마음 한편에 촉촉이 적셔드는
깊은 사연을 지닌 채

석양에 긴 그림자 드리운 길
사그라지는 노을 빛 아래
쓸쓸히 고향을 지키며
아쉬운 세월 안고 황혼에 젖는다.

A Crooked Pine Tree

Empty-minded, looking up at the sky
from the precipitous peak of a mountain,
the green pine tree gives forth a fresh scent.

Like crooked pine trees guard the family grave-site,
the tree also firmly upheld its fidelity,
even when there were torrential rain or strong winds,
even when big blizzards were on their way.

Holding a deep longing for love,
now it is as bent as the back of a shrimp.
But it still has quite a deep story
that is full of pathos.

With the long shadow cast by the setting sun,
it stands against the evening glow;
forlornly protecting my hometown,
feeling sorry for time, it's aglow with the sunset.

천내강天內江

강물이 시를 읊으며 흐른다.

전망대에서 바라보면
바위산을 휘감아 내려오는 강물이
서정시를 쓰며 흐른다.

강물위에 수많은 언어들이
은하수처럼 내려앉아 맑은 숨결로
시가 되어 흘러내린다.

낭떠러지와 돌부리를 넘어
부서진 조각들 물비늘로 반짝이며
더 넓은 바다로 흘러간다.

바람은 물을 감싸 안고
강줄기로 맺힌 언어들을 아우르며
아름다운 시를 읊으며 흘러간다.

The Cheonnae River

The river flows, reciting a poem.

I look down from the observation deck;
the river that flows around the rocky mountain,
is writing a lyric poem.

Numerous words sit on the surface of the river,
which is like the Milky Way;
the words on it become a poem, murmuring down.

Passing by the cliff and some jagged stones,
each word of the poem glitters on the ripples,
and flows to the open sea.

The wind embraces the water;
the river, putting together the words,
flows, reciting a sweet poem.

김연하(金連河) 시인 (호: 古潭)

중앙대학교 국제경영대학원 졸업
월간《문예사조》로 등단
(사)한국현대시인협회 이사
한국가곡작사가협회 이사
(사)한국문인협회 회원
한국전자저술상 수상
서울 카톨릭한우리감성상 수상
국가 유공포장 수상

〈작품집〉
시집 :『깨어나는 산』『세월은 흘러도』
　　　『인생유정』『겨울소나타』
　　　『백두대간사계』『강마을』
　　　『꽃들의 향연』『인연』
　　　『마음의 창』『아름다운 강과 바다』
　　　『가을서정』『바람의 언덕』
　　　『망향의 봄』『통일의 염원』
　　　『바다시집』
시선집(詩選集):『조약돌 사랑』『호반의 찻집』『영겁의 강』
시사집(詩寫集):『여명의 빛』『사계의 서정』
수필집 :『아름다운 인생』
시조집 :『그리움은 강물처럼』『계곡의 봄』
노래시집:『가을연가』『날아라 새들아』
　　　　　『구름 나그네』『그리운 얼굴』
　　　　　『푸른 나의 꿈』『내 사랑 내 곁에』
　　　　　『꽃비 내리네』『가슴속의 별』
　　　　　『봄날의 왈츠』『노래시전집』

About the Poet

Poet **Kim Yeon-ha** (pen-name: Godam)

He graduated from the International Business School of Chung-ang University. He started his literary career through a monthly magazine, *The Munyesajo*. He is a board member of the Korean Modern Poets Association and the Korean songwriters Association. He is also a member of the Korean Writers Association. He won the Korean Electronic Writing Award, the Seoul Catholic Prize for Hanuri Emotion, and the National Service Merit Medal.

He has published the following poetry books: *The Awakening Mountain, Though Time Goes By, Love and Affection in My Life, Winter Sonata, Four Seasons of Baekdu-daegan Mountain Range, A Village by the Riverside, A Feast of Flowers, A Fateful Relationship, The Window of the Heart, The Beautiful River and the Sea, Autumn Sentiments, The Hill of Wind, Spring of Nostalgia, The Wish for Reunification, The Collection of Poems About the Sea, The Eternal River, The Love Towards Pebbles, The Cafe by the Lake*.

He has also published two collections of photo poems, *The Light of Dawn* and *Lyricism About Four Seasons*. What's more, he once published a collection of essays, *Beautiful Life*, and two collections of sijo poems, *Longing Is like a River* and *The Spring of the Valley*.

As a songwriter, he has published the following poetry books for songs: *Autumn Sonata, O Birds Fly, Cloud Wanderer, The Face I Want to See, My Green Dream, My Love Near Me, Flowery Rain Comes, The Star in My Heart, A Collection of Poems for Songs*.

우형숙

現 국제 PEN 번역위원, 국제계관시인연합회 번역위원, 한국현대시인협회 번역위원, 한국문인협회 시조분과 번역팀장, 유네스코 문학창의도시부천 운영위원, 시조시인, 영문학박사(시번역 전공). 모교인 숙명여자대학교(25년)와 세종대학교(5년)에서 영문학 및 번역 강의(겸임교수) 후 2017년 은퇴.

〈주요번역집〉

변영로의 『진달래동산』
변영로의 『코리언 오딧세이』
변영태의 『한국의 詩歌』
김민정의 시조집 『누가 앉아 있다』
김민정의 시조집 『함께 가는 길』
유성규의 시조집 『O Poet』
최순향의 시조집 『행복한 저녁』
이서연의 시조집 『내 안의 그』
유네스코 문학창의도시 부천 시선집 『60인, 부천을 노래하다』
모나 베이커의 『라우트리지 번역학 백과사전』(공역)
정완영의 시조선집 『엄마 목소리』(공역)
이석수의 시조집 『엄마의 일기』(공역)
서진숙의 시조집 『실리콘밸리 연가』(공역)
한국현대시조선집 『해돋이』(공역)
한국현대시선집 『나의 고향 나의 엄마』(공역) 등

(E-mail: hyungswoo@hanmail.net)

About the Translator

Translator **Woo Hyeong-sook**

She is a translation committee member for the International PEN Club, the United Poets Laureate International, and the Modern Korean Poets' Association. She is a leading translator for the sijo division of the Korean Writers' Association. She also works as a steering committee member of Bucheon UNESCO Creative City of Literature. She is a sijo poetess and she holds a doctorate (ph. D) in English literature (major: poetry translation). She taught English literature and translation at her alma mater, Sookmyung Women's University (for 25 years) and Sejong University (for 5 years) as an adjunct professor. She retired in 2017.

She translated the following literary books: Byun Young-ro's two books, *Grove of Azalea and Korean Odyssey*, Byun Young-tae's *Songs from Korea*, Kim Min-jeong's two sijo poetry collections, *Someone Is Sitting* and *Going together*, Yu Seong-gyu's sijo collection, *O Poet*, Choi Soon-hyang's sijo poetry collection, *Happy Evening*, and Lee Seo-yeon's sijo poetry collection, *The Man Inside Me*. She also edited and translated *Songs of 60 Poets from Bucheon, UNESCO Creative City of Literature in Korea*. Moreover, she translated the following books in cooperation. *Routledge Encyclopedia of Translation Studies* by Mona Baker, Jeong Wan-yeong's sijo poetry collection, *Mom's Voice*, Lee Seok-soo's sijo poetry collection, *Mom's Diary*, Seo Chin-suk's sijo poetry collection, *Silicon Valley Sonata*, an anthology of modern Korean sijo, *Sunrise*, an anthology of modern Korean poetry, *My Mother in My Hometown*, and so on.

(E-mail: hyungswoo@hanmail.net)

영겁의 강 The Eternal River

초판   1쇄 인쇄일 | 단기 4354년 (서기 2021년) 1월 25일
초판   1쇄 발행일 | 단기 4354년 (서기 2021년) 2월 1일

지은이 | 김연하
번 역 | 우형숙
펴낸이 | 황혜정
인쇄처 | 삼광인쇄
펴낸곳 | 문학사계
                 등록일 2005년 9월 20일 제318-2007-000001호
                 서울시 중구 세종대로 135-7 세진빌딩 303호
                 Tel 02-6236-7052, 010-2561-5773

배포처 | 북센(031-955-6706)

ISBN | 978-89-93768-63-3
가격 | 9,000원